Dumpling Day

WORDS BY **Meera Sriram**   ART BY **Inés de Antuñano**

RECIPES BY **Laurel P. Jackson**

Barefoot Books

step inside a story

Dumpling party today in town!

Let's all cook and hurry down.

Spicy samosas point to the sky.
Didi is bringing chutney to try.

1 little dumpling on our plate now!

Apple dumplings are doughy and sweet.
Mom serves up a sticky treat.

Stuffed wu-gok is a crunchy nest.
Gor gor always fries them best.

2 dumplings before,
Then we add 1 more.
How many dumplings now?

3 !

Fufu balls are too soft to chew.
Auntie will serve a nutty stew.

3 dumplings before,
Then we add 1 more.
How many dumplings now?
4 !

Crispy gyoza is filled with pork mix.
Oji-san packs pairs of chopsticks.

Golden bourekas cool on the rack.
Saba samples the puff pastry snack.

5 dumplings before,
Then we add 1 more.
How many dumplings now?

6 !

Warm tamales are wrapped in corn husk.
Prima steams them from dawn to dusk.

6 dumplings before,
Then we add **1** more.
How many dumplings now?

7!

Shish barak comes with a tangy hint.
Baba garnishes with parsley and mint.

7 dumplings before,
Then we add 1 more.
How many dumplings now?

8 !

Pelmeni pop out of trays that gleam.
Babushka scoops thick sour cream.

8 dumplings before,
Then we add 1 more.
How many dumplings now?

9 !

Ravioli burst with soft cheese.
Bambino begs, "Can I have one, please?"

9 dumplings before,
Then we add 1 more.
How many dumplings now?
10 !

10 little dumplings and people to greet,
10 little dumplings ready to eat.

We eat and laugh and gather round,
We party till the sun goes down.

10, 9, 8, 7, 6, 5, 4, 3, 2...

And this last 1
is for you!

Let's Make Dumplings!

On the following pages, you will find recipes for all the dumplings in this book! You will need a grown-up helper to cook them with you. If you have eaten some of these dumplings before, you might find that these recipes are similar to or differe from the way you have tasted them. Every family has their own unique way of making traditional recipes. What foods does your family like to cook together?

WHAT ARE DUMPLINGS?

Dumplings are made of dough wrapped around all sorts of fillings. They can be steamed, fried or baked. People all around the world make different-shaped dumplings with a wide variety of spices and ingredients. Some are eaten before a meal or as part of a main course, while others are enjoyed for dessert.

RECIPE TIPS!

• If a recipe makes extra filling, you can freeze the leftover filling and use it another time.

• After you make a recipe, write down notes on how it turned out so you will remember what to do next time.

• For any recipes involving meat or dairy, you can look for vegetarian or vegan versions online or invent your own!

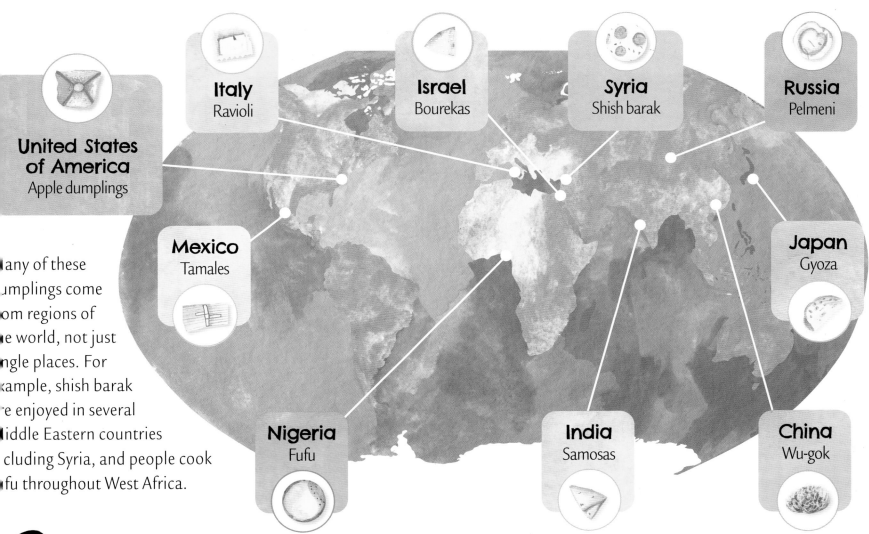

United States of America
Apple dumplings

Italy
Ravioli

Israel
Bourekas

Syria
Shish barak

Russia
Pelmeni

Mexico
Tamales

Japan
Gyoza

Iany of these umplings come om regions of e world, not just ngle places. For xample, shish barak re enjoyed in several Iiddle Eastern countries cluding Syria, and people cook fu throughout West Africa.

Nigeria
Fufu

India
Samosas

China
Wu-gok

CAN YOU MATCH THESE HELPERS TO THEIR DUMPLINGS?

Didi: Hindi for "older sister"

Mom: American English for "mother"

Gor gor: Cantonese for "older brother"

Auntie: Nigerian term of respect for grown-up women

Oji-san: Japanese for "uncle"

Saba: Hebrew for "grandfather"

Prima: Spanish for "girl cousin"

Baba: Arabic for "father"

Babushka: Russian for "grandmother"

Bambino: Italian for "young boy"

Samosas (India)

YOU WILL NEED:

Dough
8 puff pastry sheets, defrosted

Filling
3 medium potatoes

1 cup (250 g) peas

2 tsp curry powder

1 tsp ground ginger

½ tsp cumin

½ tsp coriander

½ tsp garlic salt

½ tsp garam masala

Frying
3 Tbsp vegetable oil

1. Make the filling:

- Wash and peel the potatoes. Slice each potato into 6 pieces and place them in a large pot.

- Fill the pot with cold water, just enough to cover the potatoes.

- Turn the stove to medium heat and cook the potatoes for about 15 minutes, until they are tender (easy to pierce with a fork).

- Place the cooked potatoes in a large bowl and let them cool. Then mash with a fork or potato masher.

- Stir in the peas, curry powder, ginger, cumin, coriander, garlic salt and garam masala.

2. Assemble the samosas:

- Take out one puff pastry sheet. With a knife, cut out a circle that uses most of the pastry. Then fold the circle in half.

- Dip your finger into a bowl of water and gently moisten the edges of the half circle.

- Fold the half circle over to make a triangular shape. Pinch the moistened edges together to make a cone.

- Fill the cone ¾ of the way with filling.

- Pinch the open side of the dough to close the cone. Use a moistened finger to make sure that the edges are all sealed.

- Repeat until all the samosas are made.

3. Fry the samosas:

- Heat the vegetable oil in a frying pan on medium heat.

- Place 3 or 4 samosas at a time into the frying pan. Fry for about 2 minutes on each side, then flip. Repeat until both sides are golden brown.

- Put the fried samosas on a plate lined with paper towel to drain off extra oil.

- Serve alone or with chutney, as a side dish or snack.

Makes: 8 samosas • **Time:** 1½ hours • **Serves:** 4 people

Apple Dumplings (United States)

Makes: 6 apple dumplings • **Time:** 1½ hours • **Serves:** 6 people

Prepare the apples:

Peel and core all the apples and set aside.

Make the dough:

Pour the flour into a medium-sized bowl.

Mix in the baking powder and salt, then the softened butter and pour in the milk.

Continue to mix until you have a soft dough. Use your hands!

Shape the dough into a large ball. If the dough is too sticky, add a bit more flour.

3. Assemble the dumplings:

- Divide your ball of dough into 6 smaller balls.
- Roll out one ball onto a floured surface to make a circle about the size of 2 apples.
- Put one apple in the middle of the circle.
- Wrap the dough around the apple and cover it, leaving just the hole from the core uncovered.
- Repeat until all the dumplings are made.
- Grease a deep baking dish with butter.
- Place the apple dumplings on the dish.
- Preheat the oven to 350°F (175°C).

4. Make the sauce:

- In a saucepan, mix the brown sugar, water, butter and cinnamon.
- Turn on the stove to medium-high heat and cook until the mixture starts to bubble.
- Take the sauce off the stove and pour it over the dumplings.

5. Bake the dumplings:

- Put the dish of dumplings into the oven. You may want to place a baking sheet under the dish to catch any sauce that might boil over. Bake for 40–45 minutes or until the dumplings turn golden brown.
- Serve warm as a dessert, with vanilla ice cream or (for more traditional apple dumplings) sweetened milk or cream on top.

YOU WILL NEED:

Dough
2 cups (300 g) all-purpose / plain flour
2½ tsp baking powder
Pinch of salt
⅔ cups (85 g) butter, softened
½ cup (118 mL) milk
Extra flour for rolling out
Extra butter or cooking spray to grease the pan

Filling
6 medium apples

Sauce
2 cups (270 g) brown sugar
2 cups (473 mL) water
¼ cup (60 g) butter
½–1 tsp cinnamon

YOU WILL NEED:

Taro Dough

2 Tbsp hot water

2 Tbsp cornstarch / cornflour

1 lb (500 g) taro (a root vegetable that can be found at most Asian grocery stores)

2 Tbsp butter (or coconut oil)

1 tsp sesame seed oil

1 tsp sugar · ½ tsp salt

½ tsp baking soda / bicarbonate of soda

Filling

1 Tbsp cornstarch / cornflour

2 Tbsp warm water

1 cup (150 g) ground chicken or pork

¼ cup (60 g) shiitake mushrooms, diced

¼ cup (60 g) carrots, diced

¼ cup (60 g) peas

2 Tbsp vegetable oil

2 tsp five-spice powder (also available at most Asian grocery stores)

1 tsp sugar

salt and white pepper to taste

2 tsp sesame seed oil

2 tsp soy sauce · 1 tsp oyster sauce

Frying

2 Tbsp of cornstarch / cornflour

2–3 cups vegetable oil (enough to cover the wu-gok)

Wu-gok (China)

1. Make the taro dough:

- Mix the hot water and the cornstarch to make a paste and set aside.
- Peel the taro and cut it into small cubes. Place the cubes in a pot and add just enough water to cover them.
- Boil the taro for about 30 minutes, until the pieces are soft (easy to pierce with a fork).
- Pour out any extra water, then add the butter (or coconut oil).
- Add the cornstarch paste, sesame seed oil, sugar, salt and baking soda to the taro and mash it with a fork.
- Transfer the dough to a flat surface and knead for about 5 minutes, until it forms a soft ball.
- Put the dough in a bowl and cover it with a damp towel.

2. Make the filling:

- In a bowl, mix the cornstarch with the water and stir until the cornstarch is dissolved.
- Add the ground meat, mushrooms, carrots and peas and mix well.
- Heat the vegetable oil in a saucepan on medium heat, then add the meat mixture and stir until the meat is lightly browned.
- Mix in the five-spice powder, sugar, salt, pepper, sesame seed oil, soy sauce and oyster sauce. Cook and stir for a few more minutes.

3. Assemble the wu-gok:

- Put a little bit of oil on your hands to make sure that the dough will not stick. Then divide the dough into 8 balls.
- Take one ball and flatten it out on your hand to make a circle. Now, curve your hand up to make a bowl.
- Spoon 1 Tbsp of the filling in the middle of the dough circle
- Close the dumpling by pinching the edges of the dough together to make a ball. Repeat until all the wu-gok are made.

4. Cook the wu-gok:

- Sprinkle the wu-gok with cornstarch.
- Heat the vegetable oil on medium-high heat. Then fry the wu-gok until they become puffy and golden brown.
- Remove the wu-gok with a slotted spoon and place them on a plate lined with paper towels to drain off the extra oil.
- Serve as a side dish as part of a meal or enjoy for dessert with a cup of tea.

Makes: 8 wu-gok · **Time:** 2 hours · **Serves:** 4 people

Makes: 18–30 fufu, 6–8 servings of stew   •   **Time:** 1¾ hours   •   **Serves:** 4 people

Fufu & Peanut Stew (Nigeria)

Cook the yams:

Peel and cut the yams into small cubes.

Wash the cubes and put them in a large pot. Add just enough cold water to cover them.

Turn on the stove to medium high heat. Boil the yams for 20–30 minutes, until soft.

Remove the yams with a slotted spoon and place in a large bowl, leaving the water in the pot.

Mash the yams:

Use a fork or potato masher to mash the yams, adding warm water from the yam pot ¼ cup at a time.

Continue mashing until the yams have a doughy consistency with an elastic texture (thick enough to roll into a ball).

Add salt to taste.

3. Make the fufu:

- Roll 2 Tbsp of dough between the palms of your hands to form a ball. Place onto a serving plate. Depending on how big you make them, you should be able to make 18–30 fufu balls.

- Repeat until all the fufu are made.

4. Make the stew:

- Put the onion, half of the broth, 2 garlic cloves, ginger and tomato paste into a blender. Puree until smooth (about 30 seconds).

- Place the other 2 garlic cloves and vegetable oil in a frying pan or casserole dish. Cook on the stovetop at medium heat until soft.

- Add the chicken legs, salt and pepper. Cook for 3 minutes, turning the chicken over halfway through.

- Pour the puree over the chicken and cover with a lid. Cook on medium-low heat for 10 minutes.

- Meanwhile, add the pepper flakes, peanut butter, tomatoes and the other half of the broth into the blender and mix well (about 30 seconds).

- Pour the mixture into the stew and cover with the lid.

- Check the chicken every few minutes. When oil from the peanut butter appears on top, stir it into the rest of the stew.

- Cover and cook for 30 minutes on medium-low heat, until the stew is thick.

- Serve this stew as a hearty meal. Dip the fufu in your bowl and use it to soak up the stew!

YOU WILL NEED:

Fufu

2 lbs (450 g) puna (African) yams (these are not the same as sweet potatoes)*

4 cups (940 mL) water

Salt to taste

Peanut Stew

1 medium onion, diced

1 cup (240 mL) vegetable or meat broth / stock

4 garlic cloves, peeled

3 tsp fresh ginger, grated

2 tsp tomato paste

1 Tbsp vegetable oil

1 lb (450 g) chicken legs

Sea salt and black pepper to taste

1 tsp red pepper flakes

½ cup (125 g) creamy peanut butter

16 oz (450 g) can of tomatoes, drained

*If you can't find yams, then instead of cooking fresh yams in step 1, you can mix 2 cups (270 g) yam powder and 4 cups (940 mL) boiling water for 15 minutes, seasoning with salt to taste. Fufu can also be made with other starchy vegetables or grains such as green plantain, cassava, yucca, corn or semolina.

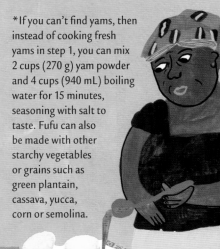

Gyoza (Japan)

YOU WILL NEED:

Sauce

1 Tbsp soy sauce

1 Tbsp rice wine vinegar

½ tsp chili oil

Filling

1½ cups (214 g) green cabbage, finely chopped

1 tsp salt

1 lb (500 g) fatty ground pork

1 Tbsp scallions / spring onions, finely chopped

2 shiitake mushrooms, finely chopped

1 Tbsp garlic, finely chopped

1 tsp fresh ginger, grated

1 tsp sesame oil

1 Tbsp cornstarch / cornflour

2 tsp soy sauce

Wrapping

1 tsp cornstarch / cornflour

30–35 round wonton or gyoza wrappers

Frying

3 Tbsp vegetable oil

¾ cup (180 mL) water

1. Make the sauce:

- Mix the soy sauce, vinegar and chili oil in a small bowl and set aside.

2. Make the filling:

- Using your hands, mix the cabbage, salt, pork, scallions, mushrooms, garlic, ginger, sesame oil, cornstarch and soy sauce in a large bowl. Set aside.

3. Make the gyoza:

- Sprinkle a baking tray with 1 tsp of cornstarch to stop the gyoza from sticking.

- Place a wrapper in the palm of your hand.

- With your other hand, dip your finger into a bowl of water and wet the edges of the circle.

- Put ½ Tbsp of filling into the middle of the wrapper.

- Fold one end of the wrapper over to make a half-circle and press the open sides together to seal.

- With the thumb and index finger of one hand, make a row of pinches across the top of the wrapper (the side facing up), so that you end up with a row of pleats like an open fan.

- Set the gyoza on the prepared baking tray (flat side down, pleated side up).

- Repeat until all the gyoza are made.

4. Cook the gyoza:

- Heat a large frying pan on medium-high heat with 1 Tbsp of vegetable oil.

- Fill the pan with 10–12 gyoza.

- Cook for 3 minutes, until the bottoms of the gyoza are golden.

- Pour ¼ cup (60 mL) of water around the gyoza and cover the pan.

- Cook for another 3 minutes.

- Remove the lid and cook until all the water has evaporated.

- Move your gyoza to a plate, golden side upwards.

- Repeat until all gyoza are cooked.

- Serve the gyoza with the dipping sauce as a starter or snack. You could also serve rice and miso soup for a traditional Japanese meal.

Makes: 30–35 gyoza • **Time:** 1½ hours • **Serves:** 6 people

Bourekas (Israel)

YOU WILL NEED:

Filling

3 medium potatoes,
  peeled and cubed

1 Tbsp vegetable oil or butter

1 medium onion, finely chopped

¼ cup feta cheese, crumbled

1 large egg

Sea salt to taste

Pinch of black pepper

Dough

1 large egg

2 large puff pastry sheets, defrosted

1 Tbsp sesame seeds
  and/or nigella seeds

Make the filling:

In a saucepan, add potato cubes and enough water to cover them by 1 in (2.5 cm).

Turn on the stove to medium-high heat and boil the potatoes for 20 minutes, until soft.

Remove the potatoes and place them in a large bowl.

Mash the potatoes with a potato masher or fork until there are no lumps.

Heat the vegetable oil in a saucepan on medium-high heat. Sauté the onion for about 5 minutes, until it softens.

Remove the onion from the heat and mix with the mashed potatoes. Let them cool for a few minutes, then mix in the feta cheese, egg, salt and pepper. (If you add the egg while the onion mixture is still too hot, the heat will cook the egg.)

2. Assemble the bourekas:

- Preheat your oven to 375°F (190°C).

- In a small bowl, beat the egg with a fork. Set aside.

- Cut each sheet of puff pastry into 9 squares. You should have 18 squares total.

- Spoon out 1 generous Tbsp of filling and put it in the middle of one square.

- Dip your finger into a bowl of water and wet the edge of the square.

- Fold the square to make a triangle and pinch the edges together. You can stretch the dough to help it cover the filling.

- Dip a pastry brush or your finger into the egg and brush all over the puff pastry.

- Press the edges with a fork to seal them shut.

- Sprinkle a pinch of the seeds on top.

- Repeat until all the bourekas are made.

3. Bake the bourekas:

- Place the bourekas on a baking sheet lined with parchment / greaseproof paper. (Alternatively, grease the baking sheet with butter or cooking spray so the bourekas don't stick.)

- Bake the bourekas in the oven for 30 minutes or until they are puffy and golden on top.

- Enjoy your bourekas warm as a breakfast food or snack.

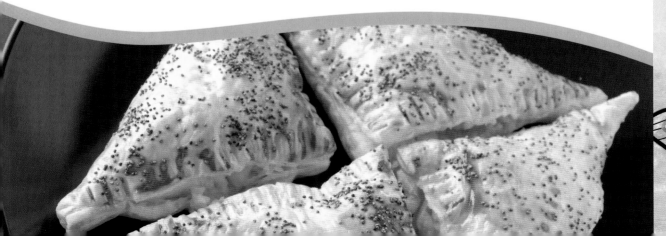

Tamales (Mexico)

YOU WILL NEED:

Corn Husks

12 dried corn husks*

Masa

½ cup (113 g) vegetable oil

1½ cups (190 g)
   cornstarch / cornflour

½ tsp baking powder

1 tsp salt

1¼–1½ cups (355 mL)
   vegetable broth / stock

Filling

1 Tbsp (14 g) butter

1 small onion, diced

2 garlic cloves, finely chopped

1 tsp salt

2 tsp cornstarch / cornflour

1½ cups (350 g) cooked, shredded
   meat (chicken, beef or pork).
   For a vegetarian filling, use a
   mixture of roasted peppers and
   cheese instead.

¼–½ cup (60–120 mL)
   vegetable stock

*If you can't find
corn husks, you can
use parchment /
greaseproof
paper or leaves
of kale or Swiss
chard to wrap
your tamales.

1. Soak the corn husks:

- Put the corn husks in a large pot and cover them with lukewarm water. Soak for 15 minutes.

2. Make the masa:

- Put the vegetable oil into a large bowl.
- Add in the cornstarch, baking powder and salt. Mix until you have a stiff dough.
- Mix in the broth a little at a time, until you have a soft dough. If your dough is watery, add a little more cornstarch. The dough will also thicken as it sits.

3. Make the filling:

- Put the butter, onion, garlic and salt into another large pot.
- Cook at medium heat and stir for 5 minutes, until the onions and garlic are tender.

- Add the cornstarch and meat (or vegetarian mixture), stirring again.
- Slowly pour in the vegetable broth until you have a thick sauce.
- Cook and stir for 5 more minutes.
- Turn off the heat and let it cool.

4. Assemble the tamales:

- Remove the soaked corn husks from the pot of water and dry them with a kitchen towel.
- Take one corn husk and place it down with the wide end facing you and the narrow pointed end facing away from you.
- Put 2 Tbsp of the masa on the middle of the husk. Spread the masa to make a rectangle, leaving a bit of husk free at the edges.
- Spread 2 Tbsp of filling on top of the masa.
- Fold one side edge of the husk over the filling. Fold over the

other side edge of the husk t
cover the filling completely.
the pointed end of the husk
underneath the tamale, leav
the wide end open.

- Tie a thin strip of corn husk
around the tamale to keep it
together. Place on a dish. Re
until all the tamales are mad

5. Cook the tamales:

- Stand the tamales upright (open side facing up) in a steamer over a pot.
- Heat the water to boiling, th
cover and reduce the heat to
- Let the tamales steam for 45–60 minutes. They are dor
when the masa is no longer s
and comes off the husk easily
- Remove the husks before ea
You can top the tamales with
salsa or enjoy them plain for
filling meal!

Makes: 12 tamales • **Time:** 2 hours • **Serves:** 4 people